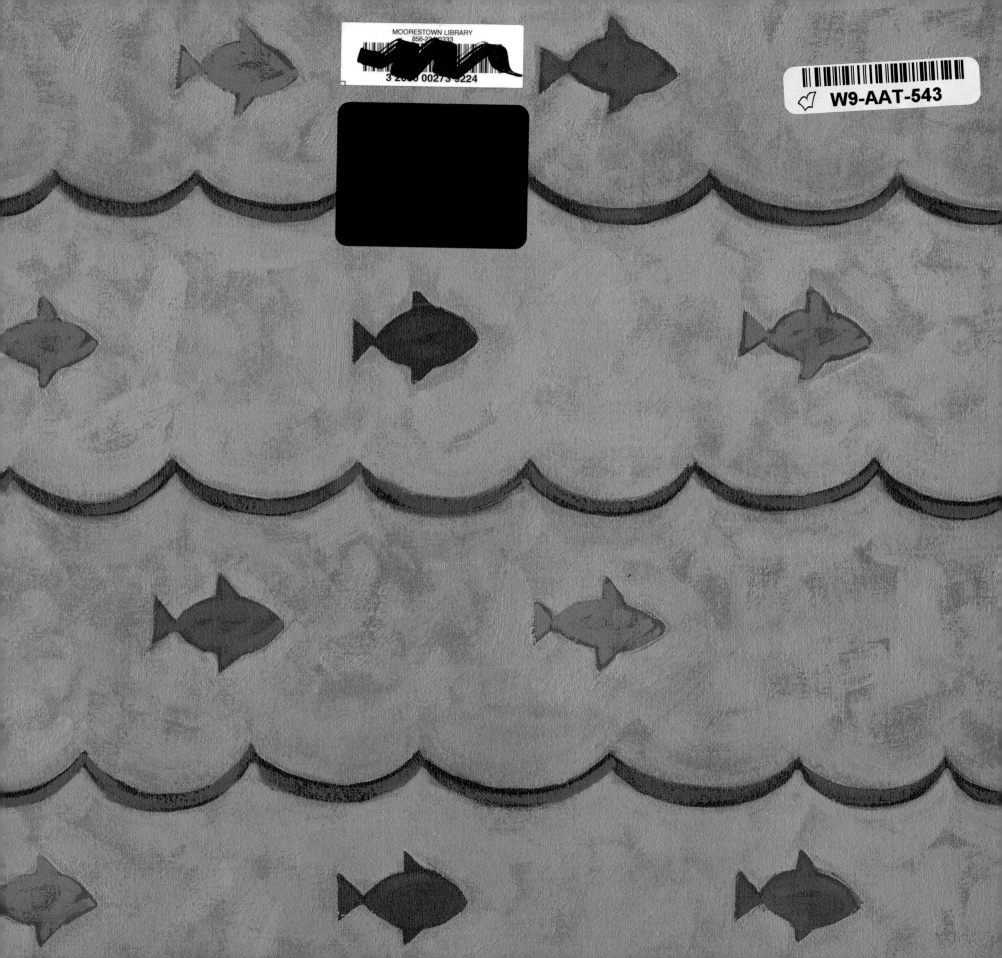

To my first mate, Jason,
and our little mutineers, Luke and Claire – M.W.

Text copyright © 2015 by Marcie Wessels
Jacket art and interior illustrations copyright © 2015 by Tim Bowers
All rights reserved. Published in the United States by Doubleday, an imprint of Random House Children's Books,
a division of Random House LLC, a Penguin Random House Company, New York.
Doubleday and the colophon are registered trademarks of Random House LLC.

Visit us on the Web! randomhousekids.com

Educators and librarians, for a variety of teaching tools, visit us at RHTeachersLibrarians.com

Library of Congress Cataloging-in-Publication Data
Wessels, Marcie.
Pirate's lullaby / by Marcie Wessels ; illustrated by Tim Bowers. — First edition.
pages cm.
Summary: A little pirate stages a mutiny to avoid bedtime.
ISBN 978-0-385-38532-9 (trade) — ISBN 978-0-375-97352-9 (lib. bdg.) — ISBN 978-0-385-38534-3 (ebook)
[1. Stories in rhyme. 2. Bedtime—Fiction. 3. Pirates—Fiction.] I. Bowers, Tim, illustrator. II. Title.
PZ8.3.W4995Pi 2015
[E]—dc23
2014029947

MANUFACTURED IN CHINA
10 9 8 7 6 5 4 3 2 1
First Edition

Pirate's Lullaby
Mutiny at Bedtime

by Marcie Wessels

illustrated by Tim Bowers

DOUBLEDAY

DOUBLEDAY BOOKS FOR YOUNG READERS

"Yo, ho, ho! Me lad, heave ho! It's time to go to bed,"
Papa Pirate told his first mate, not-so-sleepy Ned.
"But me mates are weighin' anchor, sailin' for the Seven Seas!
Can't I play a little longer? Ten more minutes, please?"

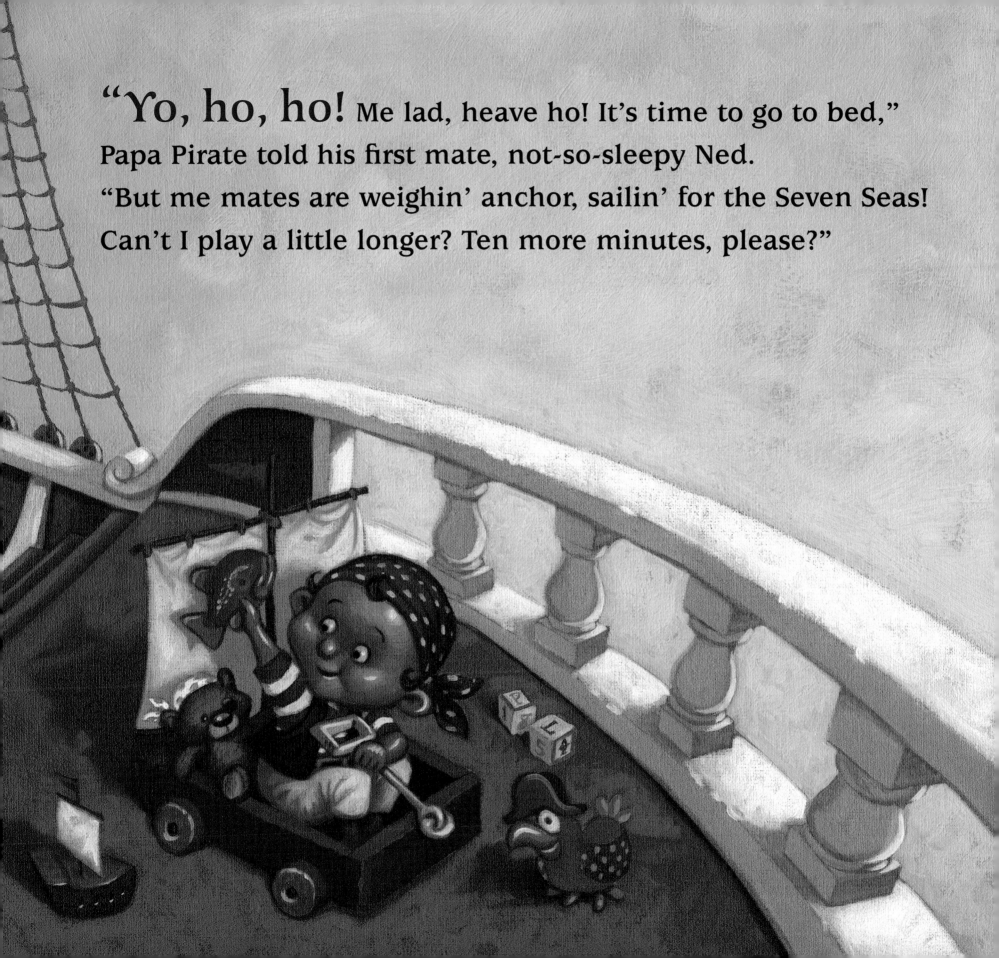

. . . stow the gear,
and lock the treasure chest.

Then we'll batten down the hatches
and get a bit of rest."

"I put away me spyglass,
me compass, and me sword.
But where is Captain Teddy?
Has he fallen overboard?"

Papa searched from fore to aft . . .

. . . and all along the bay,

until he almost tripped upon the furry stowaway.

"Here ye go now, laddie.
I have rescued yer best mate.
Let's head below and settle down.
It's gettin' very late!"

Ned shimmied up the mainmast, grinning ear to ear.
"Walk the plank to catch me," cried the little mutineer.
"Ho, ho," laughed Papa Pirate, "I'm afraid ye've met yer match!
Gotcha, little rascal. Down ye go into the hatch!"

"Climb into yer bunk now, lad. See the spot marked **X**?
Lie down and ye'll dream of the adventures we'll have next!"

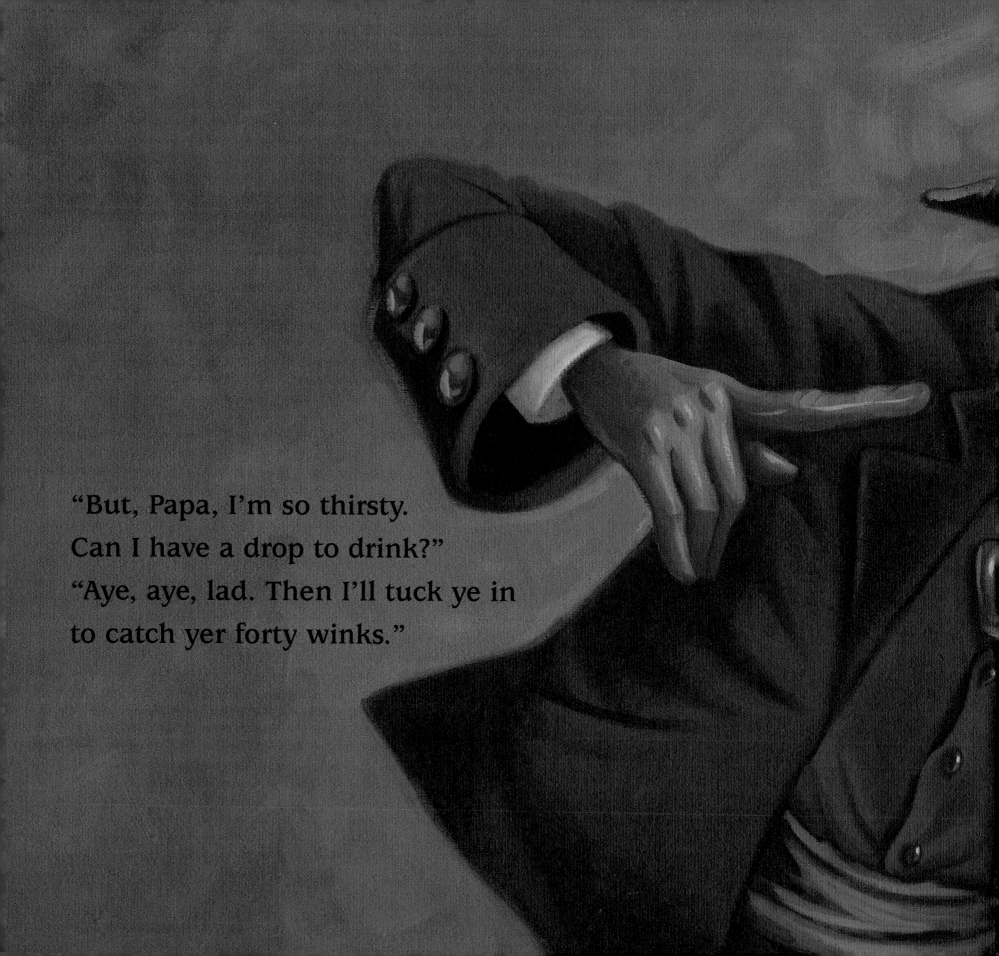

"But, Papa, I'm so thirsty.
Can I have a drop to drink?"
"Aye, aye, lad. Then I'll tuck ye in
to catch yer forty winks."

"Papa, I'm not sleepy.
Will ye spin a yarn or two?
Of Captain Jack the buccaneer
and his marauding crew?"

Papa Pirate dimmed the lamp
and fetched a comfy rocker
to tell the tale of Jack's escape
from Davy Jones's locker.

"Avast ye, lad. Yer mutiny
must now come to an end.
Tomorrow there'll be time for us
to play and to pretend.
Ye've got yer mate, ye've had a drink,
ye'll hear a bedtime tale.
Ye must be gettin' sleepy.
Ain't the wind out of yer sail?"

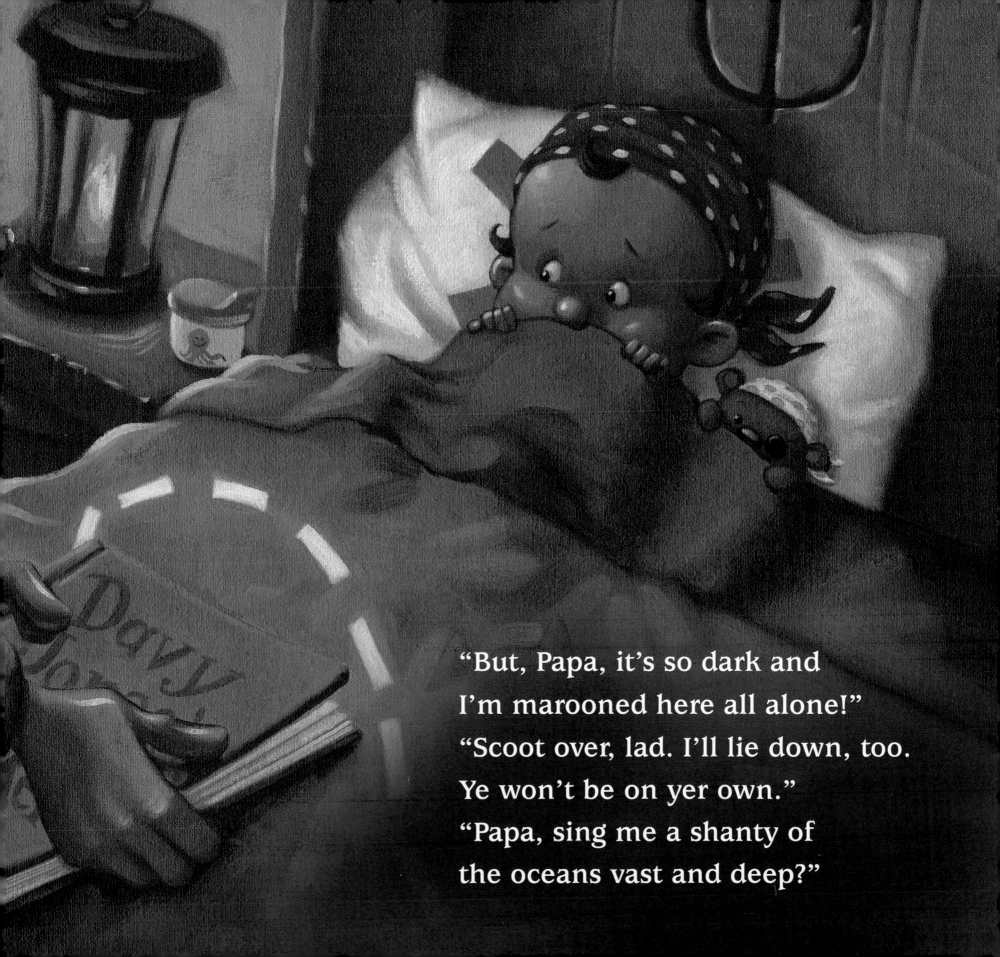

"But, Papa, it's so dark and
I'm marooned here all alone!"
"Scoot over, lad. I'll lie down, too.
Ye won't be on yer own."
"Papa, sing me a shanty of
the oceans vast and deep?"

But all Ned heard were Papa's snores, 'cause he was fast asleep!